Loppylugs

Abigail Pizer

Viking

VIKING

Published by the Penguin Group
Viking Penguin, a division of Penguin Books USA Inc.,
40 West 23rd Street, New York, New York 10010, U.S.A.
Penguin Books Ltd, 27 Wrights Lane, London W8 5TZ, England
Penguin Books Australia Ltd, Ringwood, Victoria, Australia
Penguin Books Canada Ltd, 2801 John Street, Markham, Ontario, Canada L3R 1B4
Penguin Books (N.Z.) Ltd, 182-190 Wairau Road, Auckland 10, New Zealand

Penguin Books, Ltd, Registered Offices: Harmondsworth, Middlesex, England

First published in Great Britain by
Hamish Hamilton Children's Books, 1990

Published in the United States of America, 1990

Copyright © Abigail Pizer, 1989

1 3 5 7 9 10 8 6 4 2

ISBN 0-670-83209-X

Printed in Italy

Loppylugs is a big rabbit with very long floppy ears. He belongs to a little girl called Rosie. He lives in a hutch at the bottom of Rosie's garden. The hutch is warm and cosy, lined with golden straw.

Loppylugs often sees wild rabbits
playing in the field at the edge of the
wood. They are strange and thin, and
they have funny ears that stick up.

Loppylugs longs to play with the wild
rabbits. One snowy afternoon in winter
he gets his wish. Rosie leaves his hutch
door open by mistake!

Loppylugs jumps out of the hutch. He starts to follow the rabbits' paw prints toward the trees. But the snow is deep and he keeps stumbling over his long ears.

By the time Loppylugs reaches the
wood it's quite dark. He has never been
on his own before and he is beginning
to feel frightened. Then, suddenly, the
wild rabbits pop their heads out of their
burrows.

The rabbits think Loppylugs looks a funny sort of animal, with his floppy ears and thick grey fur.

Suddenly, they all turn and scamper away. I wonder where they're going, thinks Loppylugs.

The rabbits head for a little shed at the edge of the farmyard where the farmer keeps sacks of feed for his animals. The rabbits come here in winter to nibble at the bits spilled on the floor. Loppylugs wants to help them, so he hops up and pushes over a large sack.

Crash! Thump! Down comes the sack and it spills out all over the floor. Then the rabbits hear an angry voice. The farmer is coming! They dash from the shed with Loppylugs stumbling behind.

Poor Loppylugs has never had to run
before. His ears get in the way, and he
is out of breath, and the farmer is *nearly*
on top of him – when suddenly he trips
on his right ear and flies head-over-
paws down a snowy bank. Loppylugs
has turned into a giant snowball!

Loppylugs has fooled the farmer! Flip, flap, go his ears as he shakes off the snow. He dives into a rabbit burrow to find his friends, but his tummy is too big and he gets stuck, half in and half out.

The rabbit who lives in the burrow pushes him out with a pop. Poor Loppylugs! He curls up as tightly as he can at the foot of a tall tree. He is feeling cold and hungry. How he longs for his nice warm hutch!

As soon as it is light, Loppylugs makes straight for home. He hops into his hutch. When Rosie comes to feed him she is horrified to see the open door. But there is Loppylugs inside!

'Oh, Loppylugs,' says Rosie, 'I'm so glad you didn't run away!'